A NOTE TO PARENTS

Congratulations on choosing the best in educational materials for your child. By selecting top-quality McGraw-Hill products, you can be assured that the concepts used in our books will reinforce and enhance the skills that are being taught in classrooms nationwide.

And what better way to get young readers excited than with Mercer Mayer's Little Critter, a character loved by children everywhere? Our First Readers offer simple and engaging stories about Little Critter that children can read on their own. Each level incorporates reading skills, colorful illustrations, and challenging activities.

Level 1 – The stories are simple and use repetitive language. Illustrations are highly supportive.
Level 2 - The stories begin to grow in complexity. Language is still repetitive, but it is mixed with more challenging vocabulary.
Level 3 - The stories are more complex. Sentences are longer and more varied.

To help your child make the most of this book, look at the first few pictures in the story and discuss what is happening. Ask your child to predict where the story is going. Then, once your child has read the story, have him or her review the word list and do the activities. This will reinforce vocabulary words from the story and build reading comprehension.

You are your child's first and most influential teacher. No one knows your child the way you do. Tailor your time together to reinforce a newly acquired skill or to overcome a temporary stumbling block. Praise your child's progress and ideas, take delight in his or her imagination, and most of all, enjoy your time together!

Library of Congress Cataloging-in-Publication Data

Mayer, Mercer, 1943-
My trip to the zoo / Mercer Mayer.
            p. cm -- (First readers, skills and practice)
"Level 1, Grades PreK-K."
Summary: Little Critter and his family observe various animals at the
zoo.
ISBN 1-57768-643-8 (HC), 1-57768826-0 (PB)
[1. Zoo animals—Fiction.] I. Title. II. Series.
PZ7.M462 Myg 2002
[E]--dc21
        2002008744

 Children's Publishing

Send all inquiries to:
McGraw-Hill Children's Publishing
8787 Orion Place
Columbus, OH 43240-4027

Printed in the United States of America.

1-57768-643-8

 A Big Tuna Trading Company, LLC/J. R. Sansevere Book

1 2 3 4 5 6 7 8 9 10 PHXBK 08 07 06 05 04 03

FIRST READERS

Level 1   Grades PreK–K

MY TRIP TO THE ZOO

by Mercer Mayer

 Children's Publishing

Columbus, Ohio

I am going to the zoo
with my family.
I want to see everything!

I see monkeys.
They climb trees.

I see kangaroos.
They hop up and down.

9

10

I see elephants.
They take a bath.

I see seals.
They dive in the water.

13

I see lions.
They roar!

I see ice cream.
I eat it up. Yum!

17

Word List

Read each word in the lists below. Then, find it in the story. Now, make up a new sentence using the word. Say your sentence out loud.

Words I Know	Challenge Words
I	everything
zoo	monkeys
see	climb
they	kangaroos
eat	elephants
it	seals
	roar

Capitalization: Beginning of a Sentence

The first letter of a sentence always begins with a capital letter.

Example: We love the zoo.

Look at each sentence below. Point to the letter that should be capitalized.

penguins are funny.

anteaters eat ants.

zebras have stripes.

giraffes are tall.

Zoo Animals

Point to the animals that are in the story. Try to do this without looking back at the story.

Learning New Words

Point to the pictures that have the same sound as the oo in zoo.

Logical Reasoning

Read the clues below to figure out which zoo animal Little Critter is thinking about. Then, point to the picture of the animal.

Clues
The animal has 4 legs.
The animal has a tail.
The animal is green.

Hidden Letters

Find the letters of the alphabet hidden in the picture below.

A B C D E F G H I J K L M N O P Q R S T U V W X Y Z

Answer Key

page 19
Capitalization: Beginning of a Sentence

Penguins are funny.

Anteaters eat ants.

Zebras have stripes.

Giraffes are tall.

page 20
Zoo Animals

lion

seal

kangaroo

elephant

monkey

page 21
Learning New Words

boot

broom

spoon

moon

tooth

page 22
Logical Reasoning

Little Critter is thinking about the alligator.

page 23
Hidden Letters

The letter G is near the giraffes.

The letter B is on a balloon.

The letter E is near the elephant.

The letter M is on the tree near the monkeys.

The letter T is next to Tiger.

The letter L is on the sign for lions.

The letter S is on the sign for snakes.